THE LAST PEACH

gus gordon

Roaring Brook Press • New York

5·18·19

Oh my, now **THAT** is a fine peach!

Yes, indeed, the finest!

It's the most beautiful peach I've seen **ALL** summer.
Wouldn't you agree?

I do agree. In fact, it's the most beautiful peach
I've seen in **ALL** the summers.

Yes.

Yes.

We must eat that peach at once.

We must. Let's eat it. At once!

Yes.

Yes.

Stop! You can't eat that peach!
It's the last peach of the season.

The last peach? Are you sure?

Yes, I'm sure.

Oh.

Oh.

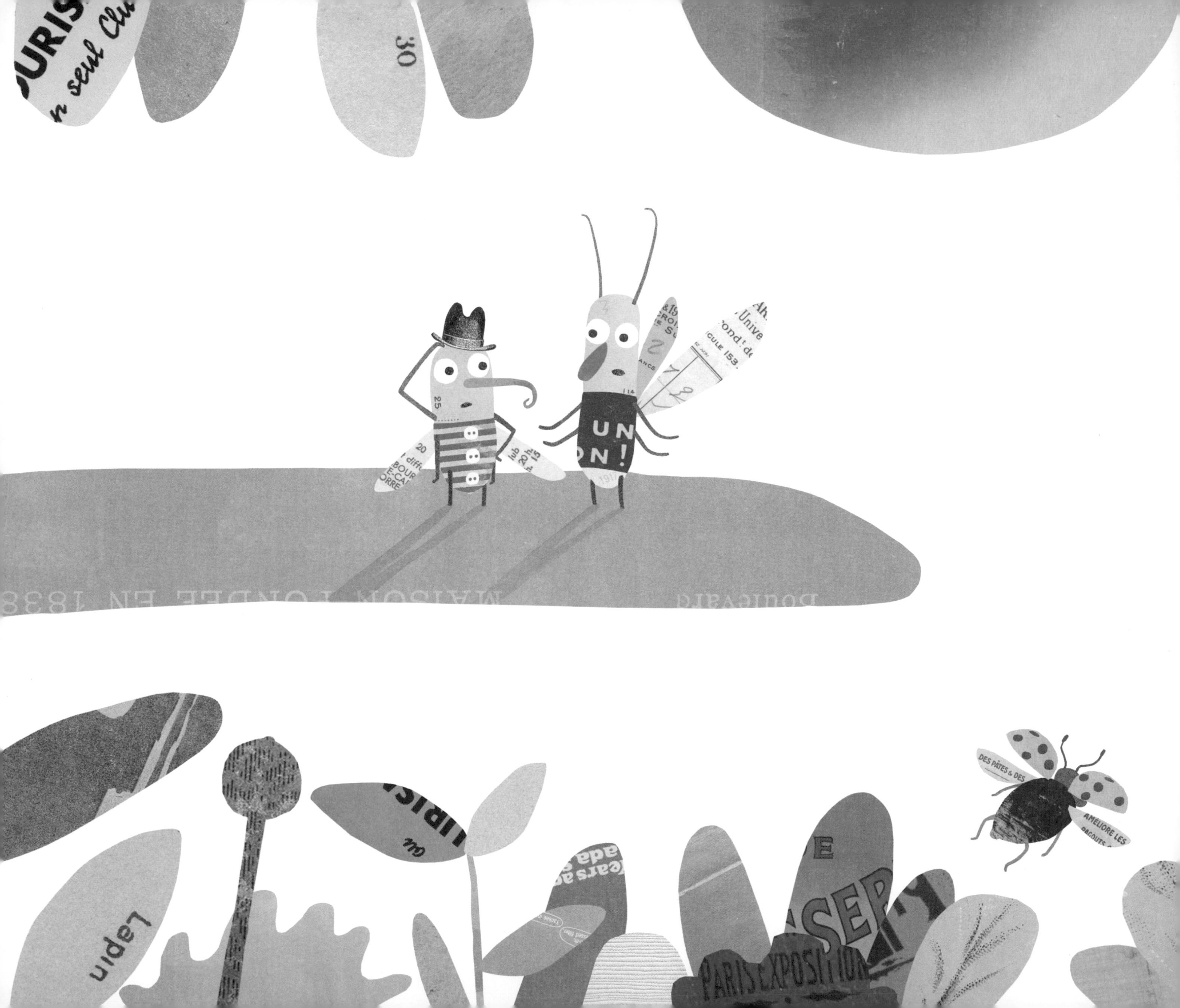
UN
ON!
PARIS EXPOSITION
DES PÂTES & DES
AMÉLIORE LES

Why can't we eat the last peach of the season?

Maybe if we eat it there will never be
another peach so lovely.

And round.

And delicious . . .

LET'S EAT IT!

LET'S!

Wait! That peach looks grand on the outside,
but you can bet it's all stinky and rotten on the inside.

Oh, no!

I'm so disappointed.

We should leave it then.

Yes.

Yes.

It's such a juicy-looking peach! What if we had just one little bite?

Yes! No one would notice, and our tummies would be very happy.

But we would probably eat the whole peach and get big tummy aches.

Oh. I don't like tummy aches.

No.

No.

It might be a magical peach! What if we ate it and could suddenly do magical things?

LIKE FLY!

YES!

Hang on, we can already fly . . .

Oh, yeah.

I have a **BRILLIANT** idea!

What?

How about we share the peach with all our friends.
They would **LOVE** us. We would be peach-hunting heroes!

We would be hungry heroes.

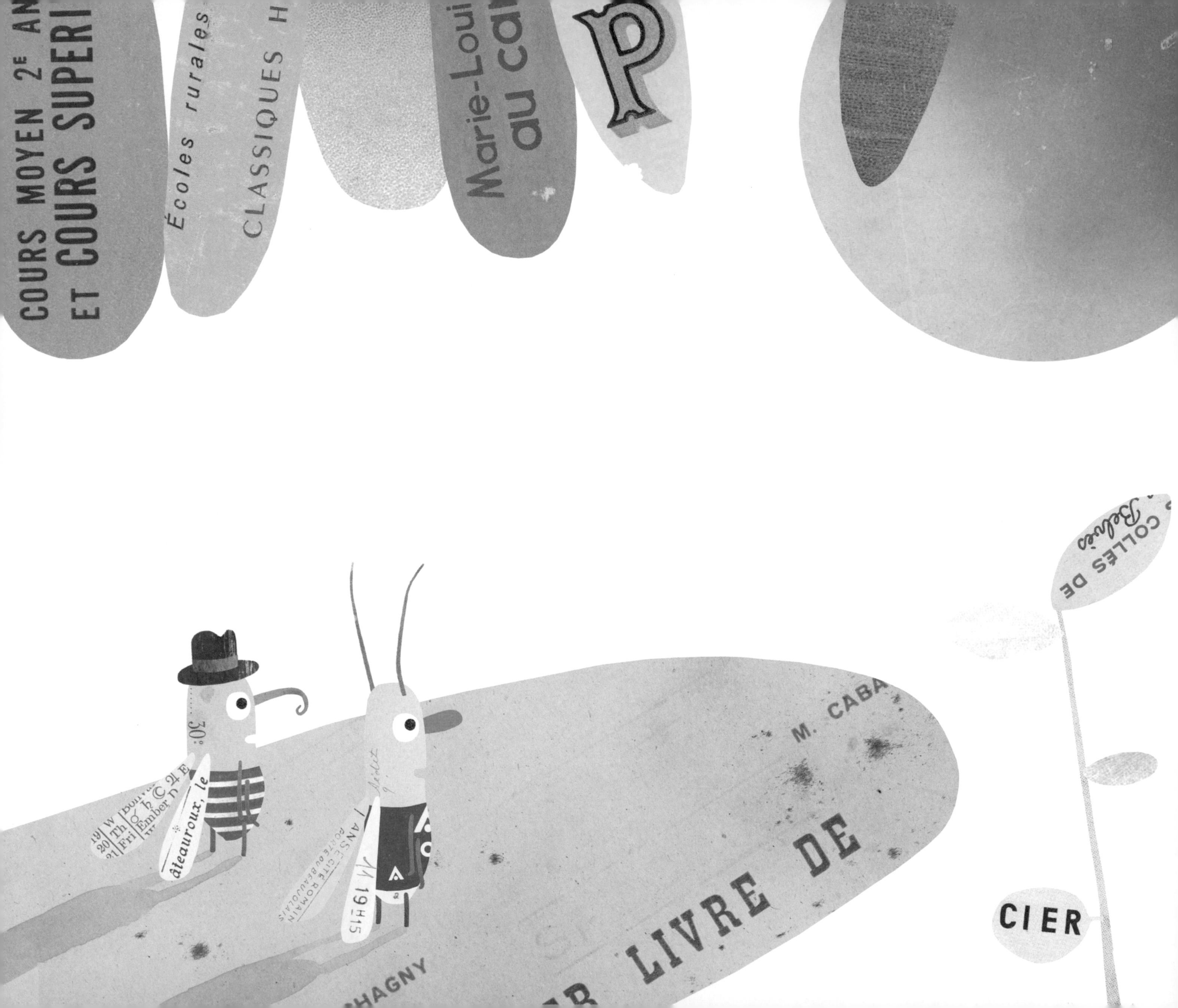

I think the peach **WANTS** us to eat it.

Yes. If it could talk it would say, "Why isn't someone eating me?"

And then we would eat it!

And it would never talk again.

Oh. Let's not eat the peach.

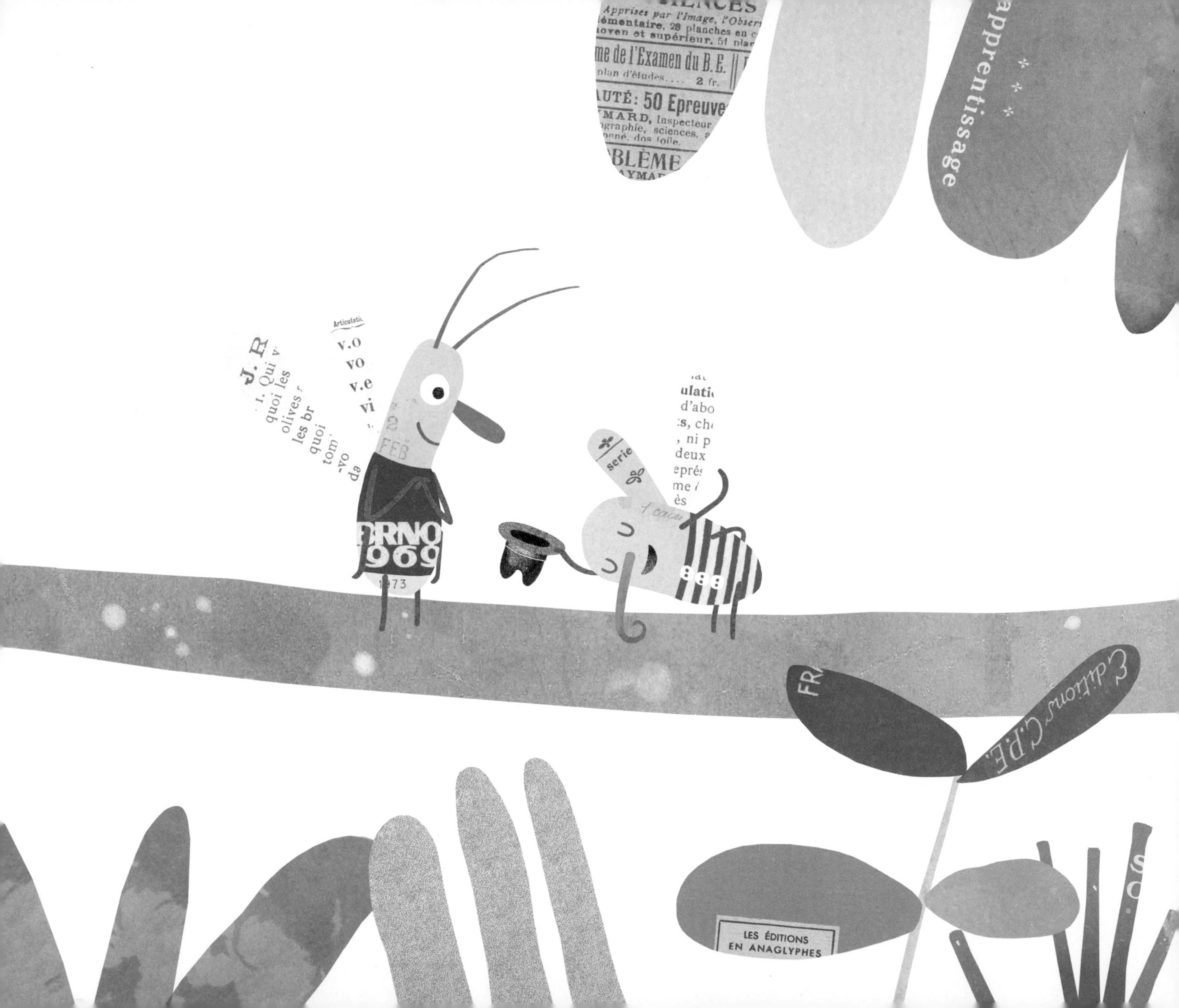

I have written a poem for the peach.

I love poems!

Dearest peach, you are the nicest of them all.
There will never be another as sweet as thee.
You warm my heart like my favorite pajamas.

That was magnificent.

Thank you.

ACTEURS
E, MALT & A n° 1
POUR LES MA
INDIQUERTRÈS EXAC
20
TIONS
LEUR
Z = S
rivière
le chemin de

I've had **ENOUGH**. I should have the peach
because I saw it first.

No, I got here first. I should have the peach.

par deux

LECTURE

That is **MY** peach!

No, it's **MY** peach!

It is **NOT** your peach!

Yes, it **IS!**

NOT!

IS!

NOT!

IS!

It is the most splendid of peaches.

You are right.

It is too beautiful for us.

Yes, it is.

Goodbye, peach.

Goodbye, peach. We love you.

9 à 17

Pour tirer tout profit de ce guide.

54.41829
Lichty Seedling

'13.

(a)

(b)

Sept 15